MATH
STICKER STORIES

PIRATES

Illustrated by Sonja Lamut

GROSSET & DUNLAP • NEW YORK

Copyright © 1999 by Grosset & Dunlap, Inc. Illustrations copyright © 1999 by Sonja Lamut.
All rights reserved. Published by Grosset & Dunlap, Inc.,
a member of Penguin Putnam Books for Young Readers, New York. GROSSET & DUNLAP
is a trademark of Grosset & Dunlap, Inc.
Published simultaneously in Canada. Printed in Singapore.
ISBN 0-448-41988-2 A B C D E F G H I J

Ahoy, mateys!
This pirate ship is ready to sail.

But the crew isn't.
They're taking a swim!
Find **5** more swimming pirates
and add them to the picture.

Now the pirates are sailing on the high seas.
Oh, no!
Sea monsters are following the ship!

A red monster comes **first**.
Find a blue monster to come **second**.
Find a green monster to come **third**.
Find an orange monster to come **fourth**.
Find a yellow monster to come **fifth**.

Who are the strongest pirates on the ship?
A tug-of-war will decide!
But it's 4 against 1.
That's not fair!
Find **3** more pirates to make the teams even.
Which team do you think will win?

The pirate captain keeps lots of pet parrots in his cabin. "Ahoy, me fine feathered friends!" says the captain. "But where are the rest of ye?"

Find the rest of the captain's parrots and put them in his cabin.

How many parrots are there now? _____

How many parrots are blue? _____

How many parrots have stripes? _____

Can you find two parrots that are exactly the same?

Land, ho!
You can help the pirates hide their treasure
on this deserted island.

Hide **1** treasure chest **in** the cave.
Hide **2** treasure chests **under** a tree.
Hide **3** treasure chests **next to** a rock.
Use the rest of the stickers to decorate the island.

Hoist the flags!
It's time to set sail
again. Find flags that
match the ones you see.
Then put them on the
empty rope in the same
order.

It's dinnertime and the pirates want their grub.
Give each pirate **1** plate and **1** cup.
Then serve the food.
Who do you think is the hungriest?
You can give that pirate the biggest helping!

Now it's time for bed.
Can you guess what pirates
dream about at night?
Put together the sticker puzzle
and see if you are right!